I read this book all by myself

....

For Philippa – LB
For Nils and Patrick – KB

RAMA'S RETURN
A RED FOX BOOK: 0 09 943939 5

First published in Great Britain in 2003 by Red Fox,
an imprint of Random House Children's Books

1 3 5 7 9 10 8 6 4 2

Set in Cheltenham Book Infant
Red Fox Books are published by Random House Children's Books,
61–63 Uxbridge Road, London W5 5SA,
a division of The Random House Group Ltd,
in Australia by Random House Australia (Pty) Ltd,
20 Alfred Street, Milsons Point, Sydney, NSW 2061, Australia,
in New Zealand by Random House New Zealand Ltd,
18 Poland Road, Glenfield, Auckland 10, New Zealand,
and in South Africa by Random House (Pty) Ltd,
Endulini, 5A Jubilee Road, Parktown 2193, South Africa

THE RANDOM HOUSE GROUP Limited Reg. No. 954009
www.**kidsatrandomhouse**.co.uk

A CIP catalogue record for this book is available from the British Library.

THE RANDOM HOUSE GROUP Limited Reg. No. 954009

Printed and bound in Singapore by Tien Wah Press

Rama's Return

Lisa Bruce
Katja Bandlow

RED FOX

It was cold outside. Winter winds blew along the pavement. Inside the house it was warm and cosy. Jaya and her mother were getting ready for Divali, the festival of lights.

"When will Daddy be home?" Jaya asked.

"You must be patient, little one," said her mother, "like the people of Ayodhya. Do you know how long they had to wait for Rama to return to them?"

"How long?"

"Fourteen years."

"That *is* a long time."

"So, while we are waiting, I'll tell you the story . . ."

. . . Prince Rama and his beautiful wife Sita had been sent to live in the forest by Rama's wicked stepmother.

Ravana, the demon with ten heads, was jealous when he saw Sita. He wanted her to be his wife.

So he sent a golden deer into the forest.
"It's beautiful," said Sita.
"I will catch it for you," said Rama. He ran
after the deer and left Sita alone.
    Ravana laughed his evil laugh. He
snatched up Sita, put her into his magic
chariot and flew away.

"Poor Sita," said Jaya. "Was she scared?"

"I'm sure she was," said Jaya's mother.
"But she was brave, too, and clever."

"Why, what did she do?"

"I'll tell you while we make the rangoli."

Jaya and her mother spread bright powders in a pattern by the front door. "This is to welcome the gods into our house," explained Jaya's mother.

"And Daddy."

Jaya sprinkled another swirl in the
rangoli. "It's very pretty," she said,
"like your necklace."

"Sita had a necklace," said her mother.
"Do you know what she did?"

. . . Sita wondered how she could let Rama know where she was. Then she had an idea. When none of Ravana's ten heads were watching, Sita slipped off her jewels. One by one she dropped them over the edge of the chariot.

"I hope Rama can follow this trail," she thought.

Rama ran through the forest looking for
Sita until he saw the giant monkey-god.

"Hanuman," called Rama, "have you seen Sita?"

"No, I haven't, but look, it's raining diamonds today!"

"Those are Sita's rings," said Rama, looking up to the sky. "She must have flown this way."

"I will help you to find Sita," said the monkey-god.

"I like Hanuman," smiled Jaya.

"He was a good friend to Rama," said her mother. "We must all try to be like Hanuman and help each other."

"What did Hanuman do?"

. . . Rama, Hanuman and an army of monkeys followed the trail of Sita's jewels until they reached the edge of the land. Far away, across the sea was Lanka, Ravana's kingdom. Rama looked at the sea.

"No human can cross that," he said. "It's too wide. How will I find Sita now?"

"I will go ahead and find Sita for you," promised Hanuman. He jumped a mighty jump over the sea.

Soon he found Sita. "Don't worry," he told her, "Rama is coming to rescue you."

"Oh, hurry, Rama," Jaya said.

"We must hurry, too," said her mother.
"We should put on our new clothes to start
a New Year. Come on."

"Is it time for Divali?" asked Jaya.

"Nearly," said her mother.

"But Daddy isn't here yet."

Jaya's mother looked at the rain
and sighed, "We must pray that the
gods will look after him, just as
they looked after Rama . . ."

. . . Rama was still looking at the sea.
"How will I get across?" he wondered.

Then the ocean god rose up. "Ravana was
very wicked," he burbled. "I will help you."
Rama bowed. "What must we do?"
"Tell the monkeys to skim stones on the water."

So the monkey army threw stones and the ocean god didn't let them sink.

Soon there was a sturdy bridge for them
to cross. This made Ravana angry.

"What happened?" Jaya asked. "Did they have a fight?"

Her mother nodded. "There was a terrible battle."

"Oh, I hope that Rama won," said Jaya.

. . . Rama and the monkey army fought Ravana and his demons for days. The demons were very fierce. Then Rama saw Ravana. He took an arrow made of sunlight and fire and shot it into the air.

The arrow hit Ravana and the
demon fell to the ground.
The battle was over.

Rama and Sita thanked the monkeys.
They travelled in the magic chariot back
to Rama's kingdom of Ayodhya.

"I wish that Daddy was back too," said Jaya, listening to the wind and rain hammering against the window. "It's dark now."

"Let's light the divas," said
her mother. "They will chase
the darkness away."

Jaya picked up the tiny lamps.
One by one, she handed them
to her mother, who lit them
and placed them on
the windowsill.

Jaya looked at the ribbons of
pretty flickering lights. "Will these
help Daddy to find us?" she asked.

"I hope so," said her mother.
"It's what the people of
Ayodhya did . . ."

. . . The people lit lamps and waved torches to guide Rama and Sita safely home.

Everybody cheered. Ravana had been beaten. Good had overcome evil.
At last Rama had returned to Ayodhya.

" . . . and look," smiled Jaya's mother, "someone else has just returned too."

"DADDY!" shouted Jaya. "You're home!"

Jaya's father came into the warmth of the twinkling lights. "The car broke down," he said. "I thought that I was going to be stuck all night, but someone stopped and helped me."

"Just like
Hanuman
helped Rama,"
said Jaya.

"Yes," Jaya's father said. "Happy Divali, everyone!"

People of the Hindu religion celebrate the New Year with the festival of Divali. They decorate the house with bright colours and lights and send cards and presents to their friends and family. You can make diva lamps like Jaya's.

Small clay lamps called divas are lit and placed in windows to bring blessings from the Hindu Gods.

YOU WILL NEED:
clay; water; poster paints; paintbrushes; a small candle

1. Take a handful of clay and knead it until it is soft. Roll it into a ball. Keep the clay wet with some water.

hole

Hindus make rangoli patterns from coloured powder or rice to welcome visitors to the house.

2. Use your thumb to make a small hole in the ball. Make the hole bigger by pushing out the sides until it looks like the picture above.

3. Make the bottom flat. Let your diva dry.

4. Next, paint on a rangoli pattern like the ones shown here. Or make up your own pattern!

5. When the paint is dry, your lamp is ready. Put a candle inside and ask an adult to help light it.

TIP: you can paint the inside of the lamp as well as the outside.

Make Divali cards for your friends and family.

YOU WILL NEED:
a sheet of thin card and colouring pencils

1. Fold the card in half.

2. Place one of your hands on one side of the card and carefully draw around it.

3. Colour in the hand shape with patterns like these.

4. Write 'HAPPY DIVALI' inside!

Lisa Bruce

Where did you get the idea for this story?
I love stories from different religions. I wanted to help children understand other people's beliefs.

Did it take long to write this story? I wrote the story lots of times until I was happy with it.

Do you celebrate Divali? I don't celebrate Divali, but I have friends who do.

What is your favourite part of Rama's story? I like the part where Sita throws her rings over the edge of the chariot to make a trail for Rama to follow. That was very clever of her.

What did you love when you were a child? I used to love winter nights with strings of pretty lights against a dark sky. I liked being warm and cosy inside by the fire.

Did you always want to be a writer? When I was little I wanted to be a fire engine driver! Now I work as a librarian and a writer.

Katja Bandlow

How long did it take to paint the pictures for this story? It took me around ten weeks to paint the whole book.

What is your favourite part of this story? I like the way Jaya is preparing for Divali with her mother. I wanted to join in too! It reminds me of getting ready for Christmas, which I love.

Did you always want to be an illustrator? Until I went to art college I didn't know there was such a job as an illustrator! I've always liked to draw and paint and I love being an illustrator.

Who is your favourite character? I think Jaya is my favourite character, along with her cat. I like the way she asks all the questions I would like to ask.

What do you like to draw most? My favourite thing is to doodle while people talk. Starting to draw and not knowing what will be there at the end is lots of fun!

Will you try and write or draw a story too?

Let your ideas take flight with
Flying Foxes

Moonchap by Mary Murphy

All the Little Ones – and a Half by Mary Murphy

Jed's Really Useful Poem by Ragnhild Scamell and Jane Gray

Jake and the Red Bird by Ragnhild Scamell and Valeria Petrone

Pam's Maps by Pippa Goodhart and Katherine Lodge

Slow Magic by Pippa Goodhart and John Kelly

Rama's Return by Lisa Bruce and Katja Bandlow

Magic Mr Edison by Andrew Melrose and Katja Bandlow

Rosa and Galileo by Anne Cottringer and Lizzie Finlay

A Tale of Two Wolves by Susan Kelly and Lizzie Finlay

That's Not Right! by Alan Durant and Katharine McEwen

Sherman Swaps Shells by Jane Clarke and Ant Parker

Only Tadpoles Have Tails by Jane Clarke and Jane Gray

Digging for Dinosaurs by Judy Waite and Garry Parsons

Shadowhog by Sandra Ann Horn and Mary McQuillan

The Magic Backpack by Julia Jarman and Adriano Gon

Don't Let the Bad Bugs Bite! by Lindsey Gardiner

Trevor's Boat Hunt by Rob Lewis